Jet Stream
a short telling of a long story

Rush Tully

ISBN: 9781728711188

Jet Stream
a short telling of a long story

by

Rush Tully

for my brothers
Robert, Nathaniel, Joseph

Prologue

I am a window. I used to think you got something for being a window. But you don't. Just the window. Some people are doors or walls. You're more of a wall, or maybe a supporting beam. Me, I'm a window, and not even that – but a window way up in the attic, where no one goes, and becomes the voice of reason that keeps the house from burning down.

Life is not linear. It goes up and down, back and forth, in and out of the house. You might have a marriage on the second floor. It wanders into the basement where you have friends. Occasionally you are sitting in the garden. A corporeal summation. Why would you ever say there is a beginning or an end?

Time is an oscillation. It travels while simultaneously holding its breath and is neither here nor there but bent on finding something it can't quite remember. Perhaps what it ate for breakfast. Some sour milk and dry toast.

Into the middle we are born. Of families, of centuries, an hysterical, generational chaos from which for some reason we wish to escape. We think. The window. We jump. But the center is gone and we must speak in longer sentences, we must forget what came before because it didn't and we must love everything mustn't we, because the window is sliding down the side of the house into the gutter where it is washed out to the center and never began, again.

It's all still there – the people, the angels, the miscreants.
I can't lie for them anymore. They are what they are.

Visit

There was movement, and there was direction. We are mostly unaware of these things, but the destination always knows what's coming to its cry. And all destinations remain in the desert. The desert instructs us as to the meaning of intent.

José Luis Montaño and The Texas Two-Step swam along in the great sky, through clouds and sun. The atmospheric excitement was their joy. Almost, within itself, the infinite expanse of all existence. Perhaps a lesser infinite, but a provisional vision such that understanding and compassion followed behind the exquisite, thunderous moments of enlightenment. Those moments when purpose is revealed into the dark matter that longs for brightness, longs for sight, longs for hope.

This was a simple radial.

Two-Step and José had moved here before. Always a human thing. Something sensed in a voluminous haze of insensitivity. In the great call and answer they rode upon the present prediction of need and flew east, into the rising future.

They had been in Chicago enjoying Chagall's American Windows. But you know how it is when people need things and they live in "America". Ever everything right now, though not to worry. There are many angels and many pins with which to sew up the fate of God.

And they had precipitated Joseph's protection before. He was one of their easiest assignments. He was simply an artist. Actually, the ancient artisan, awoken by presence, given voice by that which will prepare each meal consumed and each sacrifice made to sustain the table set.

The most difficult thing about existing toward one plane of awareness and needing, while blackened with exultation at one's own clarity, to become in another, is precisely that need. Landings are hard to negotiate - promotions are essentially non-existent, though I have never understood why anything might be essential that ultimately ends up completely elsewhere.

This movement requires one accede to the 2nd most level of pervasive stillness while adhering to speed of such magnitude all the universe faints. The Texas Two-Step and José Luis Montaño were well practiced in the process. So it wasn't time until they presented in the park – two policemen. And since one size never does fit all, Two-Step was very large and José was very not large. They walked across the grass to where, a brief distance from the two-story, marble stone Town Hall & Courthouse, under an "as always" tree sat a solitary figure, alone in time. He was naked.

"You've come inside again," murmured Texas.

Joseph looked up and said nothing. He felt it unnecessary to speak to those who could read his mind. He did smile though. It was always a welcomed thing, to be noticed. It made him feel useful.

"Consider the sun," said José.

Joseph looked up, peering through the green, red and yellow leaves of the various fall trees. He couldn't see it, either the sun or the concept.

"Oh, good God!" Two-Step said. "You always say that, and he never gets it. Nobody gets it! I don't get it!"

"Well, I do biggie fig," said José calmly.

"Joseph, where do you like to be?" he asked.

Joseph was working hard. He thought he already "was". And "somewhere". He did like being and somewhere in the same sentence. So, since he was, he didn't move.

"Time's up," said Two-Step, latching on to the quicker spheres, ever so slowly slowing time. It disappears 'round the bend, an inflexible weave of polymorphic desire. "Goodbye and God bless," it says, as each death triumphantly reveals the greater latitude of a long held belief in good penmanship. They disappeared. Joseph frowned and they reappeared. He laughed and they left. He farted and they came back, a look of some consternation on José's face.

"Consider the sun," José pleaded.

Joseph stood slowly like a Yogi coming unglued from his shadow and began to skip across the grass over an empty busy street where he opened a door between the coffee shop and bookstore to be no longer visible in the two-story, red brick edifice that filled the block across Main St. on the south side of Town Hall park.

....

Consider the sun, whose light begins in a shallow star, proceeds to all direction forever. What is the utility of such light? Where is it? It is in different places different things. We ask the sun for life. Here on earth. So love will be in our hearts. Here prayer is answered. Tomorrow we must ask again for the light is never still as it sweeps darkness out to the center. Life includes beyond our grasp and we keep moving, following the logic of the sun. (Theme)

Between

I first became aware of Joseph one Saturday afternoon in 1953. I often accompanied my father on the bi-monthly rounds of his properties, which amounted to nearly half of what had grown to be our small town in upstate New York.

There, across the street from Town Hall Park, on the south side, was my favorite of all these. The street out front walked slowly past the warm, whimsical welcome of a five & dime, corner café, ice cream parlor, and antique vendor and, of course, the coffee shop and bookstore, between which stood a subtly expressed invitation for any to note, and inexplicably few to accept.

This trip, my father reached to open the door and found it slightly ajar. We stepped inside. I followed him up the narrow wooden staircase, polished and luxuriant from decades of wear, hundreds of feet, not all of them human, tumbling up and down without care or purpose other than to rise into the air 16 feet, stumbling back again. I was always surprised by the cacophony of smells delineated into specificity for my, as yet to be, embattled memory. My grandmother's attic, the sweet smell of the floor at the five & dime, years of sweat now comfortable in the cab of my grandfather's rusted out, old green pick-up. There was an impending emptiness that freed the mind to think clearly about the important nothings that create each day.

All this came softly into the melodically persistent counterpoint of my child-sized thoughts as we climbed the stairs, which went deep into the building, up to the second floor, finishing 10 feet from the back wall. From the landing the room moved left and right to solid walls 60ft away. Behind us the old plank floor ran to the façade up front overlooking the street. Along it were situated 5 great windows, 10 panes each in vertical rows of 5, a reminder of the Japanese mysticism incarcerated in our town for most of a war my parents would seldom talk about. Until I was older I thought humanity had experienced one fractured moment of insanity at its best. I didn't occur to me that the II implied a I, or that the dark was always there, always would be though we be armed with time and need.

The back wall held the same window pattern. But whereas the front glass was merely dirty, allowing a natural light to filter in, at the back the windows were covered over with some dark substance imitating paint. The space seemed much as it ever was, a hollow, grateful vesicle, afloat in time, saved only from sinking by the opportune existence of my father's building.

I peered around as my eyes became accustomed to the lesser radiance. Always when I came here I had an acute, pressing sense of expectation as though some wonderful truth long secret and hidden was about to show itself to me. Only with my father I felt this. As if reason were present, and absolute, denied to no one, even 6yr olds who loved the world and thought power was an abstraction lost within the limitations of mediocre minds.

Today was different.

"What do you think?" he asked.

I had been here before. I noticed no change. It smelled the same. I looked more carefully.

"What do you think?" my father said quietly.

Suddenly I realized there was no sound. Usually you could hear the cars on the street down front. You could hear the humming and gurgle of the building, cash registers, the clatter of dishes, people talking in the shops. Sound was muted here but mostly there was a lot of it.

And no edges. They were gone. I couldn't see the walls. The windows were floating, translucent and bright above the floor. I felt it, but didn't understand where it was. No upper limit.

"How are you doing?" again my father, but this time directed out, across somewhere, away from us.

"I've come home," a voice responded.

....

I think, for the most part, life happens to those who show up. We ask to come. We are invited to come. Things are happening all the time. When you show up they happen to you. If you want to understand, look around. Think. Something will occur to you.

....

It occurred to me my father knew the voice we heard. But he didn't respond and continued gazing thoughtfully into the shadow. After a few moments he turned and we left quietly back down the stairs.

A beautiful fall day had drifted in, the earth tilting itself so the light had changed its cloth from green to red, yellow, orange.

I wondered about my father never having used or rented that space upstairs. It was the only one of all his properties that had remained empty from probably before I was born. Back then I didn't know my parents came from somewhere. Everything was one thing in one place. My mother and father were an exceptional and intensely common witness to my life, though other people knew me. It was an intimate knowledge. It meant Mrs. Sotto Voce always had my favorite ice cream, a scoop of chocolate and a scoop of vanilla, waiting in a cone for me when I came in the door to her shoppe, which is where my father and I went next.

....

I never went to school. People taught me whatever occupied their thoughts at the time. My mother talked to me. My language and etiological skill became slightly eccentric. I took everything personally, though I kept this to myself. I had respect for reason as the logic of nature. Stuff over there didn't interest me. Stuff here interested me a lot. The old man who sat outside the five & dime told me I was "one who spend much time." I think I didn't go to school because of what happened to my sister. She was there already when I came. When I was old enough to dream I began to think of her often, of how she moved, how she disturbed the color of our joy. She got very excited and couldn't sleep or she seemed very tired and couldn't move. She'd be up nights upon days upon nights, convincing my father there were raccoons in the attic. She ate all the cheese and fruit and peanut butter he left in traps on the roof outside. My mother thought sometimes she was afraid of the dark and sometimes she was afraid of the light. She took her to Dr. Coughlin who said she was manic-depressive. By the time bipolar came into use, she'd been dead for 30yrs.

She fell off the top of the house in the middle of the night during a snowstorm. She had climbed out the attic window and was trying to reach the big maple tree that came up beside the house. She always said I could just hold out my hand and it would give me syrup for my pancakes. My mother found her next morning on the back step where she crawled up to sleep with our cat, Ghost. He was a very big, weird cat. He followed my sister everywhere she went. All around the house. To the store. Even to school. He slept in her bed and didn't get up until she did. No one else could get close to him. When my sister died he stopped eating and slept under the maple tree in the snow. Three weeks after, he disappeared.

For my sister, having seen the resolution of what can not be more than incomprehensible, there had been two paths by which she could arrive at the next moment, both of them less travelled, so either what is left escapes slowly into the darkness of indiscernible light. Death, inexorable and chatty, comes soon. Or all the love one soul can fathom is gathered unto a great height and hurled erratically, violently out to an inescapable future, holding, for our love, the hope what might have been is intercepted, forcing back to sanity the real truth of things.

My mother accepted both precocious exigencies and kept me close. She didn't want me anywhere away from her. Me, I was just angry. – As if there were some reason for our multiplicity of languages other than to avoid misunderstanding, I foolishly believed had there been an accurate name for my sister's condition, there would have been a serendipitously corresponding cure. After all, in the beginning was the word that fixed everything. – But the word has become nothing more than the white noise of exponentially increasing vocabularies. So better to focus on the grain of sand. Listen to silence. Then an answer will come.

It was at this point my father began taking me on his rounds, and I discovered Joseph had space while he discovered I had time.

Visit

Every angel knows truth is found solely by accident, digression is all the law, and the speed at which such beings precipitate permits the accurately random movement necessary in the pursuance of this goal. It answers, without patience, a small, satisfying degree of success. Angels have everything, now and then.

Two-Step and José were looking at Alsace-Lorraine, all of it, when it dawned upon them from the east they were needed in the park! So just for fun they needed themselves the long way 'round and needing to overshoot the park by twice the distance to Paris came back bounced off Mt. Saint Helens before needing to anticipate the '60s at County Rd E into the squad car moving south past the country lexicon of humility in architecture and came to a stop on the west side of Town Hall & Courthouse Park. There they presented themselves out of the black and white, acknowledging the redactive reciprocity of judgment, walked on over to the "as always" tree beneath which Joseph sat. Again, nothing remarkable about nudity to the police.

"What have you done with your family?" demanded José.

"What?" said Texas, staring at the pigeons pooping on the Court House.

"What have you done with your family? It's a simple inquisitive, provided you are. On a scale of difficulty, 1-100, it's a 17."

"What?" said Texas, now looking at Joseph.

"There are these families, little short-related-things running around in trivial space, talking constantly about the whether or not. What have you done with yours?"

"What?" again from Texas, looking at José.

"What! What! What! You could be more helpful. I mean you're big enough to have measurable mass. You ought to do something more with it than floating around saying what, what, what..........and why are you wearing that t-shirt?"

"What?"

"Free the Stooges!"

"I'm thinking of a number between 1 and all the rest." Said Two-Step, "It's the littlest. Like you."

The Texas Two-Step was looking at the pigeons again. Joseph was laughing. José had disappeared.

"Where does the sun live?" asked Texas.

Joseph, considering how pleasant he felt, thought it must live right there with him.

"That's correct," said Two-Step, and José reappeared.

"Did you ask him?" he asked.

"Yes. And furthermore, did you know that if you get all the human beings together for a picnic next week, stand them up, give each one a hot dog and a coke, tell them to shut up? The whole bunch will fit inside here to Swenson's farm, up to the pig sty at Galt, over to Ma Jenk's hardware in Gideon and back here."

"What's your point?"

"Well, things don't take up much space. There's a lot left over. We could
        give some away."

This interested Joseph, that space might be available. Space was his best
thing, though only because he liked it. And he had just been thinking
about where to put all the picnic tables. How would the ladies get
through the crowd with the food? The band stand. Some people think a
picnic can do without music. Classicists have music without picnics, an
oversight of graciously revelatory consternation. It reveals to us each
presence begetting its reflection, a balanced, asymmetrical sensuality
existing to both come and go. Each <u>with</u> is eternally <u>without</u>. All music <u>is</u>
a picnic to <u>which</u> the world <u>is</u> invited. <u>With without is which is</u>. Logic
becomes a useless thing. The joy of space is forever.

So easy this, Texas wept, José Luis Montaño danced an extra league,
Joseph got more space, accepting his smile on its return trip, gracefully
upset himself from the ground below, skipped over the grass, across
Main St. to sweetly up the invitation.

....

The shortest distance between 2 points is the disrupted one. Otherwise
we have difficulty measuring it. Since that's all we do well – as well as
being irrelevant – sometimes we have to disrupt a perfectly good
universe in order to have something to do.

So it is with family.
In the distance between our definition of it and the love it can engender,
there is a constant disruption while we measure and think and mostly
guessing define our need. Just like the angels, we need to be somewhere.
(variation)

Between

Initially my father and I stayed only a short time over the shops on Main Street. My father asked Joseph if he was all right or if he needed anything. How he was feeling.

But Joseph never wanted anything. It seemed he always felt good. I never understood whether he did normal things, ate or slept, though there were often wonderful smells of fresh bread in the air around us. He always only wore a baker's apron and had a wooden spoon in his left hand. There was music, not that I recognized, but beautiful. It made everything more beautiful. I thought it came from me, but couldn't understand how that would happen. I wasn't stable. Observations, awareness, tangible all inside of me. I didn't reach. I wasn't afraid. I kept hold of my father's hand.

Our 3rd stop the windows had taken on an amorphous, introspective appearance, they were unsettled, anxious. If I moved towards them they disappeared. There were pieces of light everywhere, far away. I couldn't see Joseph or my father.

"Go to the light," my father said, and let go my hand.

My father trusted people a lot more than my mother. Actually, what she didn't trust was God or nature or the universe. She was afraid of inevitability. Her best quality was the anger with which she met the world. No one was allowed to suggest what she might do with her intellect or talent. Anyone foolish enough to try began a shunning of such intensely voluminous integrity it carried through several dimensions. She erased you from her memory.

"Go to the light," my father said.

Then I was darkness, moving to the light. But I didn't move. One of the pieces came and found me. A man with colors and a brush touched the dark around him. He pulled light out of the darkness and put it somewhere I could see. It was hidden underneath my eyes. Then it wasn't. The painter hummed, reaching in and out of the darkness, everything becoming color and sound. He talked to someone, about the fine weather, what should they have for lunch. He had built a machine for flying and knew why we felt better eating spicy food with garlic, onions, olives, peppers, sweet food like grapes, peaches. A woman stood in front of him, some light he found in the darkness.

"Do you like my smile?" she said.

He laughed, turning to me.

"Do you see a road winding down the hill there? Run to the village over the bridge and bring us some bread and cheese. You're expected. Some red wine and olives would be nice too. And some fruit."

The man and woman had a lot of energy. Behind her I saw a road, water, mountains. There was a stone bridge over a river where I thought the town must be.

In the village people were everywhere, laughing, waving their arms and talking very fast about time, yesterday, that soon all the earth would be near to them because the man with the brush was going to fly. People would be kind. One of the women ran off and came back with a basket full of bread, cheese, olives, fruit, wine.

"Tell him we're waiting!" she said. "Soon we will dance! Come with if you can!"

I hurried back up the hill. The man had set down his colors and brush. He and the woman were looking at each other. I was very happy. I noticed more light come from the mountains.

"Thank you," the woman was saying. She turned to me, "And please stay for lunch. I know your father won't mind."

The woman spread a blanket on the grass. I noticed when we were not moving most of the light came from the two people. I was light.

"You're a lovely young man," she said.

The man looked at me, thoughtful, kind and began laughing. Then we were all laughing. I jumped up and began skipping like Joseph coming across the park. Then was in the space upstairs with my father.

"What is that place?" I asked.

"A window."

"Where?"

"Everywhere else."

My father said something to Joseph and we climbed down the stairs to the street and, as always, the ice cream shoppe. Mrs. Sotto Voce was usually talking to her mother when we came in. Her mother had come to live with her and help out around the store. I didn't understand when they talked. Today I did. Her mother was saying she worried about me, but now I had a nice smile and it made her very happy.

"Has he come back?" Mrs. Sotto Voce asked.

"Yes," said my father.

"A blessing," she said. "A great blessing."

....

Many people expect love exists only within the limits of imagination. That it's appearance can be understood.

I was never clear who knew that Joseph lived in my father's building on Main St. with his stories as I came to call them, and his friends, the policemen in the park. But people said things like Mrs. Sotto Voce's "great blessing." On the east side of the square was a bakery and a bar with pool tables, a small stage with a lady who took her clothes off. The old man who sat outside the five & dime said sometimes Joseph went there to dance with her in his baker's apron. I began to understand people were aware of a whole lot of things. They just didn't go on about it.

After we left the ice cream shoppe, my father walked across the street to his office in the courthouse while I went east on Main as it rose adventuring a quarter mile to the edge of town, and our house on Sheard. My mother let me do this alone because she could see me coming up hill from the kitchen window. I climbed the back steps, pushed open the screen door. There she was humming, keeping an eye on things, stirring up a batch of cookies in a new sunbeam mixer she bought at the hardware. The hardware store was on the north side of the park, beside a grocer's that had it's own butcher and a drugstore with a soda fountain. Behind them was the school I didn't go to. Kids there hung around at the drugstore after class. I preferred Mrs. Sotto Voce's ice cream shoppe and Joseph's stories.

I sat down on a three-legged stool by the kitchen sink, watching my mother pat out cookies on a big aluminum sheet. Oatmeal, my favorite. She always put an extra egg in them. That was good for me. Lots of raisins, and walnuts we picked from a tree in the neighbor's yard next door.

"Have you ever been to the space where dad talks to the man in the baker's apron?" I asked.

"Your father's property? What did you see?"

I told her about the lady with the smile and the man who showed me all the light. She set a sheet of cookies in the oven. I followed her into the living room.

My parents had a lot of books resting in high, dark, built in book cases all along the south and north walls. To the left sprawled my mother's grand piano for whom she sang and wrote music. To the right stood my father's writing desk covered with manuscripts, drawings, pens, pencils, rulers, notebooks, an abacus and hour glass, slide rule, usually a mug of gone cold coffee – a reading lamp – a picture of my sister. Behind us held the fireplace, nine mystical Hopi katsina dolls, tihu, standing across the mantle. I liked the clown best. To one side was a collection of antique crosses, some wood, some iron, running ceiling to floor – two leather chairs. On the piano sat a sculpture of the Buddha. Four tall floor lamps stood around the room on wood floors, a 10ft ceiling. There were stones and shells gathered from places before I was born, places I didn't know. Zuni and Pueblo pottery, a figurine of a woman with children and birds sitting all over her, colored glass sculptures, my father's arrowheads. A 14x7, gray, pink, brown Navaho rug lay over a couch in front of the big picture window in the wall facing east. Two songbirds in a cage sang to the light where my mother and I sat looking at a large, heavy book she had fetched from a shelf. Opening it, she placed the volume on my lap.

"Is this what you saw?" she asked.

I stared at the picture for a long time before I realized my mother had gone back to the kitchen. When she returned I saw her smile and felt her hand placed on mine.

"Everything, from the smallest part of an atom to the greatest star, is a story," she said. "The finest among us throughout time are the story tellers. The man in the space is one of these." After a moment she added, "The rest of us keep a record."

....

It never occurred to me to question placement of the things I was invited to see. Time and space require no reason in their prescience. They are the protestation of all logic, the catharsis of doubt. My father's property above the shops held no limitations. Alone, things to do.

"Come back when you're ready," my father said.

I discovered myself standing in front of a cave. It opened back into a wall of stone. Trees and bushes grew up and over it. There were flowers on some, different colors. Around the entrance women and children were cooking at several fires. It smelled like my mother's oxtail soup. A little girl jumped up, ran over to me and took my hand, leading me to one of the fires.

"This is my friend," she said. "Can I show him the stories?"

"Don't get in the way," one of the women answered.

I could see for a while after we were in the cave. Then it was a little dark. The girl kept hold of my hand until we came to a wide cavern where several men up on ladder branches were drawing red, yellow, black colors from the walls. They held up clumps of moss and hair that glowed, pulling light to it from the rock. Some men were blowing brightness into the dark with hollow pieces of bone. Older boys stood near them as they worked, holding up cups of flame, like candles or torches. The girl stood watching as a giant black bull began moving through the stone. She reached over, picking something off a ledge of rock and handed it to one of the men.

"He needs more light!" she said excitedly.

"You are my light!" the man laughed. "One day you will bring all the stories!"

The little girl grabbed a torch from one of the boys and we raced off down another passageway. Animals were everywhere, pushing, leaping, chasing stone away from the light. Bulls, buffalo, big lions, birds, a bear, rhinoceros with fur, reindeer, people's hands, bows, spears. Everything was moving. We ran as fast as we could, the rock and stone ahead of us.

Across meadow to hide behind trees edged between colors of wood and tall grass.

The little girl jumped up and down, crying, "I'm free, I'm free!" Then she turned and said very seriously, "We have to get more color for the light." She was only 3 or 4. We walked along a path, past animals breathing quietly in the stone, into the mountains. The girl had dried meat. She showed me what seeds, nuts, berries to eat, what water to drink. We walked for 3 days until in the forest we met a group of men who gave her tools and colors, told her what animals to make. She gave them reindeer hides and mammoth rugs. After they were gone she turned to the man on the ladder of branches and showed him what she had brought. He knelt before her, holding out a candle, said –

"You are my light."
"This is you."
"You are this."

The little girl took back my hand. We walked out of the cave. Sat with the people there and had some of my mother's oxtail soup.

"Life is very big," I said to my father.

"Yes," he answered as we descended to the street for ice cream, one scoop chocolate, one scoop vanilla waiting in a cone.

....

For several years I went every two weeks to visit the storyteller. He and my father were always somewhere off to my left, speaking quietly, occasionally looking over to me as I wandered around in the light. It was everywhere. It came from everywhere. It came as darkness to the pieces. I never got tired. I was in the desert. A woman took me there. The rain had come, stretched the dust into red sand, opaque and running close to truth, translucent that even the sun became a dark thing, yet shining black as blue, yellow, orange, pink leapt praising the wisdom of luminescent skulls looking down from an ocean of ecstasy, hidden somewhere beneath the woman's thought.

I didn't understand this. Everything was so fast. But the woman spoke to the darkness very slowly, explaining why it must change, why it could not lie. It was like this every time I went to the pieces of light, speed; but distance made it slow.

....

One afternoon I talked to a man with a green apple on his nose. He said it was the apple Eve had chosen in the Garden of Eden. He said that to make a choice was to create love, and that love was God. We sat on a wall talking for a long time, watching the ocean, the gray clouds.

....

A man moved dark lines of ink upon the approaching light while notes flew everywhere around a great hall with huge rugs hanging on the walls, beautiful white, gold, shiny dark wood furniture, ornate chairs, small tables, settees, writing desk, closets, a ceiling 20ft in the air covered with the color of flying angels, animals in the forest, people lying on flowers and bathing in fountains. Windows cascaded from ceiling nearly to the floor, thick drapes completely. Children ran through the notes, grabbing handfuls, giving them to the man as he sat on his stool. He played a piano, shouting and laughing, ordering the notes to calm down long enough to speak songs, voices, instruments, all at once in a thunderstorm of misunderstanding pushing us to peace, sunlight. A woman called that he was to hurry and finish storming around.

"Supper is ready!" she yelled. "The children are invited to join us!"

From the dining table we could see her bringing big plates of fruits and cheeses from her kitchen – bread, roast chicken, spaghetti, vegetables, wine. The whole time notes followed the man, jumping and sailing around him, while he talked incessantly. He told us how much fun it was to be alive, how silly and ridiculous were people, so no wonder there was so much thunder and lightning running about.

....

Each day after my father took me on rounds to his properties, after my ice cream, my mother, with a plate of cookies, went into the living room and showed where there was a record of what I had seen.

Sometimes I climbed up to the window in the attic and sat, watching the maple tree. I saw its numbers, its water. Its breath. It held up the sky, peered into the earth.

But things go wrong. I think it was my fault. I fell in love.

You think you know something. There are things over on your left, on your right. You don't understand both are true. The heart is this drum. It counts out time. I fell in love, fainted, lost consciousness. I was ill.

You are never what you are until you are. Then we all understand. The darkest trinity climbs the stairs to question reason. Obscuring hope, it falls so near the window is lost. The depth of light, responding only to love, I fell.

Visit

Two-Step was enjoying the N.Y. subway. The constant, variable rhythm of sound. He closed his eyes, which an angel can't actually do since its mind is always open. The rhythm spoke. Clarity, confidence, convivial joy, Christ-like chromosomes, consequence, calcification (not that), cerebral cortex, coexistence, celestial, catharsis, cholera (nope), colonitis (this isn't helping), class warfare, castration (sweet Jesus in a baby blanket) – simultaneously, or close enough, José spoke,

"It moved," he said.

"What do you mean, it moved?" intoned Two-Step. "What moved?"

"The thing that wasn't moving."

"What wasn't moving?"

"How should I know? It was supposed to be there already."

"So!"

"So why is it still moving? Secrets are not good for people."

"Who cares? We're angels."

.....Texas and José were easily distracted...../\.....reverting briefly to an electro-magnetic pluralism so as to enjoy white water rafting on the Colorado River, misplaced the ironic shift between an emotional disconsequence and universal id, overshot the park, found themselves in an office at Town Hall & Courthouse.....

"Of course, there are no mistakes," said Two-Step.

The two were looking at pictures on the desk when a man walked in. Looking from the pictures to the man, José asked,

"Where's your little boy? Is he with Joseph?"

"Joseph *is* as always," the man said.

Percolating off the *tutto il posibile*, José and Two-Step found Joseph *was* as always – in danger of omniscience among the over dressed.

Texas spoke,

"...the square root of nothing is round, while πr^2 indicates that triangulation is more than inadequate to sum up the seriousness of laughter, after all, a square is but two triangles dancing round about somewhere in Nepal, simple Mesopotamian irrigation, when the mathematicians, who believed that things do add up, defeated the You-fraidies, who believed things don't add up, drove them across the river to the chaos of gesticular construction in a 3rd absurdity, 1st being retro-gravitational thought, 2nd, future perfect of a babbling brook, earth became a better vacation destination..."

"You believe that?" asked José.

Joseph didn't believe in anything. He understood certain things to be accurate, therefore true. And the reason this is true is the same as the reason it's not true – because.

"Did you know?" continued Two-Step, "that if you take the following statement, A>B, circumnavigate the sun, at 90° it becomes A=B, at 180° it becomes B>A, at 270° B=A and home again. Thereby proving that there is a set A, which is greater than or equal to set B, which is all other sets B through gazillion, such that each set other than A is greater than or equal to A, and everything else. This is known as the *Simplicity and the Complexity*, where of, the *Simple* is *Complex*, and the *Complex* is *Simple.* We are in S. People in C. Much less interesting key. A minor is acceptable at parties."

Joseph thought this was obvious. Another of those things he didn't have to waste time believing in, or, as nothing comes first, out.

"The sun!" said José.

"...the sun..," interrupted Texas, "...is inextricably sewn up for/by/with/in mathematics as it pulls into utility the darkness of light. We are the children...

"Family," corrected José.

"...the children of the sun and are also inextricably sewn up for/by/with/in mathematics as we harvest that utility..."

"I thought you said you didn't get it," said José.

"I lied," replied Two-Step.

Joseph was already half way across the park, skipping along to Ravel's *Bolero* as he inextricably translated himself up *'the everlasting good on you'* to its related peace & quietude.

....

Consider the sun. It radiates infinitely in all direction throughout moment. Yet, only once will it stop to chat with the infinite commitment of all perspective. So it is with all manner of thing, the greatest star to the loneliest particle. The sun is married to the light; we are its children. God with us as we seek alone ourselves with God, the lightness of the dark, the darkness of the light. (Variation)

Between

One of our wonderfully optimistic Saturday mornings my father recounted the overseeing of construction for Town Hall & Courthouse by his great, great Grandfather Paul. Design based on a series of drawings by Grandpa Paul's wife, Mae.

Abutting Henry George St. on the north side of the park, the building faced south, surrounded by spruce, tamarack, red oak strolling through the grass into the neighborhood. The adventure was interrupted only on the S.E. corner, Main & Lewis, by a stand of trees, the governance of which was left to the large population of red delicious apples hanging from its branches.

The hall was built of brilliant white, almost translucent marble that held blue, green meanderings of color. Orange-brown stains, hematite, oxidized by unrelenting, time-honored miscalculations of weather, peeked out at their own exposition to light. A 3ft parapet ran cheerfully around the top. The whole structure was smooth, plain. Simple.

As I walked up three wide marble steps, nine foot oak doors were open in welcome to the park residents. Inside, four great schoolhouse lamps hung in an atrium space vaulting thirty feet into the air. Across, heavy stairs, lightly stained, rolled up eight feet to veer left/right to the long walkway circumscribing the second floor. The only decorative aspect anywhere in the architecture, an ornate, black, wrought iron railing, three feet high, running along the walkway back down the stairs to the first floor.

Our mayor, Mr. Thimble, and his secretary, Mrs. Heartfeldt, had their office to my left with my father's office behind running under the staircase to the back wall. Mrs. Heartfeldt was the real boss of our town. She even told my father what to do sometimes. He would tell her to talk to my mother. My mother and she were good friends. They saw the sense of everything, except going to church. My mother was eleven when she announced to her parents there were no people at the Methodist church intelligent enough to instruct her as to where things come from, or belong. Her mother and father continued to take her to church, but while they were at services she escaped from Sunday school across Lantern St. behind the building to the bowling alley, 3 blocks south of Main, where she spent her allowance on Baby Ruths and thought about where things really come from. She thought bowling balls were very interesting.

All the town hall offices had frosted glass in the doors, with name plaques next to say who was inside. And large, double hung windows, muntins for upper panes, the wood, again, lightly stained.

The desk in my father's office was larger than his at home, but less cluttered. Instead, the clutter was on two long, narrow tables under the west windows. Book cases were full to spilling, journals, papers, his collection of stuffed animals to whom he gave his various lectures, talks, advice before passing it on to the general public. Pictures covering his life until now filled the remaining wall space. As in the living room at home, he had the same picture of my sister on his desk. And one of my mother and me. He was standing at one of the tables looking through The Complete Works of Plato when I came in. I had run all the way, so was out of breath.

"Mom said I'm supposed to tell you to invite Dr. Steiner's new nurse to supper tonight," I managed.

"Actually, she's in the office," he said, looking up. "You could run upstairs and ask her for me."

Dr. Steiner's practice on the second floor took up the whole back wall with his office, two examining rooms, and reception waiting area where Dr. Steiner and his nurse were also the secretary. He didn't have appointments. People just called him, then came over if he said to. Or he went to their house. The nurse started her day at the school two blocks away, to see if any kids should stay home. To rest up for learning I think.

I raced upstairs, crashed into the waiting room, stopped still...

(I was brave, silly, twisted, logic, passionately blind, uncaringly gentle, nervous, sure, scared, dizzy – these things taken in all sense – I stood my ground, waited at death's door, prophesied attention. I let go of hope, squandered my love. I didn't know anything, expecting victory. There was tension in my stance. There was beauty in my imbecilic determination, I could not stop...)

I thought she was one of the pieces of light come from the darkness. An explanation gushed out of me, all about the stories and the man in the baker's apron who was a friend of my father's.

"I can show you," I said. "And my father told me to ask you to dinner this evening."

"That would be very nice. What time should I be there?" she asked.

I didn't know, raced downstairs to my father's office and back up.

"Mom says to come at five if you would."

"That is lovely," she confirmed.

What else should I do? I wiggled about, left, came back, left, told my father her answer, ran up the hill and asked my mother what was happening to me.

....

Our dining room was from the kitchen through a butler's pantry. Built into all three were mahogany cupboards, glass windowed doors, drawers, polished, green mushroom glass pulls, cast iron fleur-de-lis pulls. My mother and father loved things that didn't leave.

In the center of the dining room a round, Stickley Bros. table of quarter-sawn white oak floated silently on a thick wool, 8x12 rug from Nepal. My mother had shown me where it came from in one of her books, pictures of the people who wove it, symbols and patterns through which they spoke. It was joined by four Talavera place settings, several Majolica serving platters and bowls. When we had company and extra leaves for the table, my father sat at the far end. Behind, snug against the wall, a Limbert side board served its purpose. Our linens and silver from Europe, to which my parents had sailed with their parents when children. The families had known each other from the time my father was seven. Into this friendship my mother was born eight years later.

....

Kathryn was taller than my father, dark, distinctly there. She shone intently, inwardly, vis-à-vis source. A cloud of soft thoughts, ideologies, an invisible rhythmic abeyance swirled about her as she moved.

All through supper she spoke excitedly, the symmetry of unknowns, geometry of water, the colors of light as they illuminate simple Persian gardens, heaven on earth.

There, lying upon Achaemenidian carpets, Ferdowsi, Rudaki, Khayyam as they supposed spinning words of darkness into being. Tonbak, daf – dotar, seter, tanbur – ney flute. Nothing is lost.

My father and I cleared the table and began washing dishes, leaving my mother and Kathryn to talk and laugh, holding each other 'til they cried.

"I have not known your mother happy for a long time," my father said.

"Am I a story teller?" I asked, watching Kathryn.

My father looked at me quizzically,

"What a remarkable question," he laughed. "All I can tell you is some people are afraid of story tellers. They're too accurate."

After Kathryn left I climbed up into the attic, sat by the window looking at the maple tree as it wandered far away, sleeping in time.

I thought of a man I had seen bringing light as one of the stories. He sat on a wooden stool looking into the darkness. He had fiery white-silver hair, lots of it, coming out his ears, nose, eyebrows. He turned to me and I was very still. I had never seen eyes so devoid of movement. I saw peace, an absolute, kindness I didn't understand. He was listening. Suddenly he turned away. His eyes began to pull numbers and symbols from emptiness, faint at first, then hotter, glowing until they burst forth, waiting.

"It's a bunch of numbers!" he cried. "They don't know where they belong! They need you to play with them. Watch. Push them around. Put them here and here."

He had his arms stretched out, pointing in opposite directions, then took off, flying around, around, around, laughing. It was a very bumpy ride, but he grabbed handfuls of numbers, stuffing them together into tiny balls, which he ate.

Then he burped.

Dozens of asymmetrical pictures, in perfect balance, flew out onto a window. Etched into glass as symbols, lines, numbers, letters.

"Beauty is everything," he said. "Make something beautiful, something becoming away until you can't see it anymore."

I thought he was beautiful.

"Would you like a twinkie?" I said.

"Since I don't know what that is, I think I must have it," he said.

He ate the one I gave him, then asked,

"Are there more of these tiny miracles?"

"Yes sir there are," I said. "I'll get some."

I turned to run back home, then stopped.

"How do I come back?" I asked.

"Just choose," he smiled.

....

"Don't be a nuisance," my mother called next morning as I bolted out the back door and down the hill to my father's office. He laughed when I told him I needed to go upstairs to see Dr. Steiner.

"Kathryn is over to the school," he said.

I plundered the stairs up to where Mrs. Blouster, too, waited for Kathryn. She had brought little Rick and Carol, her baby. Little Rick had a runny nose, a cough to go with it. Mrs. Blouster was nice. It was in her yard we gathered walnuts for my mother's cookies, two of which I brought in the black, worker's lunch pail my dad had given me, along with bologna, miracle whip, lettuce sandwiches on raisin bread – my favorite. That, and a thermos of milk I thought a fit meal for the person with whom you are in love.

But Kathryn didn't come.

....

Across Emelie St, on the west side of Town Hall Park lived our train station. Made of treated 2x6 cedar, 5 steps, 3 boards deep, 9ft wide, 8in high, wrought iron hand railing either side, black, were pulled up by a wide cement loading dock as it condensed around the long, one story building sitting there. It showed off pale green for a soft, brown trim. The south side windows lifted flower boxes above the dock, filling them with dozens of red and pink geraniums. Begonias yellow red white pink waved, bowed east. In the cold, shopkeepers planted winter evergreens, strung lights 'round the seasonal levity of arrivals and departures. Two sets of tracks ran past the dock on the side opposite steps. Twice a day a passenger train came through, south at 9:00am, north at 5:30pm. There was a freight line stop at 5:00am and 11:05pm. Whenever anyone had a train to catch they'd simply say, "I'm going to Emelie this morning." People seldom went north.

Kathryn left Dr. Steiner's at 8:30am, walked over to the station. She was visibly upset, trembled holding a letter in her left hand. Roy Potter had delivered it the previous afternoon. Mrs. Hulda Potter operated the train station along with post office there behind the ticket windows. Muntin windows east, west, south allowed a beautiful light to wander into the waiting room, whose walls were covered with photos of the town and trains circa WWI back into the 1800's. Across, leading out to the loading dock, an ornately carved, wooden Dutch door, painted red. Seven old, well worn church pews attended diligently by, hoping for travelers to whom they might confess. When not delivering mail, Roy helped his wife with train comings and goings, luggage, plumbing. He was an excellent carpenter, knew a good deal about electricity.

Kathryn purchased a round trip ticket to Brooklyn on the morning's train. Mrs. Potter wondered if she could help. Kathryn just said no, everything would be all right.

....

An adjoining space on the north end of the station, weighed heavily down by the stuff of eternal nonsense, a police department inhabited by Chief Berto Majorca, 4 deputies, Rick Bishop, Clancy Maine, 2 angels, 5 cluttered desks, numerous green blackboards, filing cabinets, files, papers, bulletin panels, challenged the thought that life could not be messy and simple at the same time.

Berto, though Greek, was a throwback to English propriety, carried neither his badge nor gun, was a mystifyingly prolific and competent gardener. He spent days eloping with his thoughts through the shops and neighborhood, around the square. Rick and Clancy presented a more austere face to the public. They drove, armed, in a cruiser to everywhere they thought no harm might come from their crusading presence. The angels were not called upon to keep the corporeal peace. Their approach to physicality was philosophic, purely out of the blue, between itch and scratch.

Two days later Kathryn returned from the city. She found Chief Majorca playing at his desk with a plastic pinball game he bought earlier in the day from Vageli Pattos, whose fortune in life was to own the five & dime on Main St. Actually, Vageli had given the toy to Berto. Giving things away was something he often did. He was alone in the world, considered the town's people his family. He spent a great deal of time sitting with the old man in front of his store, quietly gazing at the sun as it gave them the warmth of competent thought, conversation, friendship.

....

After talking to the Chief, Kathryn walked up hill to see my father. I was sitting in the dining room working through a geometry text as my mother had told me to do. I wondered why she kept supper late. I wondered why Kathryn seemed to know my parents deeply. Though it didn't bother me at all, I wondered why people knew a lot of things I didn't.

The grownups ate in the kitchen, but I could hear some of the conversation. Kathryn was terrified my father would be angry with her over something she had done. He said that was nonsense. I heard my mother say she mustn't worry, that things happen for a reason. Everything would be all right. Afterward, my parents walked her home to a boarding house on Pope St., a block past the school.

....

I began to get how things are in a serious relationship. Sometimes people are not available. They have things to do. You need to go in the same direction and not make suggestions. That's the love part. Following around and listening is the between part. It's hard to tell the difference.

I often found Kathryn sitting on the grass under the apple trees at Lewis and Main. We spread our lunches over the woolen blanket she always brought, looked at books, read magazines that told our fortunes. We shared thoughts, ran errands, had adventures. We walked over to the Post Office if we felt like it. Kathryn sometimes had a letter that hadn't been delivered. But if she did she never read it, just folded it up and put it in her pocket. She didn't look like a nurse. She didn't wear a nurse's uniform. In our town people dressed however they wanted. You needn't ask what they did. We visited Chief Majorca if he was in his office. Or he visited us when he was out for walks, always sitting with us awhile, asking how we were doing. I liked him.

We went to the grocer's on Henry George. The Cortlandts had a lot of fresh vegetables from Chief Majorca's garden. Mr. Cortlandt was the butcher. He had lamb, specially brought from Albany for Kathryn to make her tagines. Kathryn called him Robin. She brought spices back from the City for his wife, Dev. Berto, Vageli, Mrs. Sotto Voce and her mother, Mayor Thimble and Mrs. Heartfeldt, even the policemen who talked in the park to Joseph – they all came to our house when Kathryn and my mother decided to cook.

Of course, Kathryn and I could always run across Main to the five & dime where Mr. Pattos had a Zero bar for each of us. One for the old man in front of his store.

Beyond, out of the ordinary, more than adventure, a profound endeavor. This was hanging out at the train station, waiting for trains that never came, believing one day they would. Hiking through woods beyond our hill, looking for signs of life as though it wasn't all around us, pretending we were different than rocks, trees, water. Taking time to examine every item in the five & dime, thinking for Franz's hardware on the other side of Town Hall, examining need, wonder if we had different names would we live someplace else.

....

Two months after Kathryn came back from Brooklyn, under the apple trees, we noticed across the park on the train platform a man staring at us. After several minutes he walked down the steps to Emelie and toward us. Kathryn watched him come. She was very still, alert, then stood up spoke quietly,

"Let's go."

We left our things on the ground, walked quickly over, into the five & dime to stand by the cash register where Vageli sat on a high stool resting his elbows on the counter. He watched Kathryn as the man entered. The old man stepped softly in behind. Vageli called out cheerfully,

"Hello sir! You know, you're most welcome to come on in and visit. With me. I just love the company. But leave my customers alone."

Still cheerful he reached down, pulled a gun off a shelf, set it on the countertop. The man laughed.

"Ah, no worries. Just having a bit of a wander. You sure have lovely weather up here." He left, nodded at the old man on his way out.

"Come back anytime!" Vageli called after.

Kathryn phoned Berto. Shortly, the two policemen who talked with the storyteller came in their squad car, drove us up Main to our house. They didn't come in.

Next day my father took me down to the park. I sat with Kathryn on Town Hall steps while my father talked with the policemen and Joseph under his "as always" tree. The man stayed several days going into shops around the square, talking, taking pictures. He tried to go up to the stories but there was a padlock on the door, a sign reading, "No Trespassing."

betwixt

(...perniciously average, so clarified an ignorance, three leagues into oblivion, they approached the world with a repressive diplomacy, mesmerizing in its self-righteous calm, a puissant hopelessness, this redolent wrist-ringing prevarication, chronocidal, wonderless, weightless, no muscle, gravitas, cryogenically preserved egos bullied through the delicate clostridium of an ossuarial maze, bistrolic pedants sewn into the inadequacy of quantuumless, ill-begotten pestilence – 3rd generation English royalty, saving the infidel, they lived in Brooklyn, were artists with a weapon, an art gallery in Chelsea...)

I didn't like Kathryn's parents. They smiled a lot. They scared me. I couldn't see them. They had insisted Kathryn bring the storyteller, his work to their gallery for display. Kathryn cursed them quite fluently in a language they couldn't understand. They sent the private detective to our town. He returned with little more than a great deal of rumor. Though Clive and Edna Stilting were intrigued to hear Joseph's outside/in was born of a perception profoundly indifferent to their own.

And as some perversion of law may easily claim this sacred distance be its own, the Stiltings convinced themselves that, with some delicacy, Joseph could be manhandled through a system of lies that might pronounce truth an incestuous sweetheart. They hired an entire law firm. There came a summons. An appearance must be made at Brooklyn County Municipal Courthouse, Thursday, 14th day of February 1957. A reply politely informed, all were welcome, 2nd floor Town Hall in the Park, Judge William Breklandt presiding, Wednesday, 14th day of August 1957. The padlock remained on the storyteller's door. My father stopped including that property on his rounds.

"Is this my fault?" I asked.

"No."

"I'm the one who told Kathryn about the storyteller."

"This isn't about him," my father said. "This is about people who are afraid of death. Kathryn has been aware of the stories for a long time."

I didn't understand what was happening. A terrible sadness everywhere. I thought if people knew about the stories it would go away. I couldn't find Kathryn, walked down to the five & dime, asking the old man for advice. He was thinking, something he often did. I went in the store and got a Zero bar from Vageli, one for the old man. I was waiting for him to see me, when he spoke,

"Everything is somewhere." Then he laughed, opened his eyes.
"And it's moving," he cried.
"You have time. Don't waste feeling sorry for yourself." He accepted the
    Zero bar.
"Thanks for nothing," he said, very seriously and touched his heart.

I began having dreams. That I existed everywhere. At first it was in water. I dreampt there was a pond in our back yard. At the bottom was an island where all the forest animals lived. Deer, raccoons, rabbits, squirrels, badgers, weasels, otter, fox, woodchucks. They were all babies, like me. I was their friend. They trusted me. But I told someone and I was swimming down to tell them not to be afraid. They would still be safe. As I moved through the water, breathing, I saw. I am a girl. I am exactly me, my thought, my energy. I existed in the air, sometimes in earth. I am eternally me. I am an appearance.

I stopped going to the ice cream shoppe. I went to the drug store soda fountain on Henry George St. I went to the school, to Emelie. To Gridley's Pool Hall where the old man told me the storyteller and Kathryn went to dance with the lady who took her clothes off.

On the morning of August 14th Clive and Edna Stilting arrived with 3 lawyers and the private detective who in their limousine doubled as chauffeur. They parked illegally on Emelie, walked across the park past the "as always" tree, up the three marble steps of Town Hall. Mr. Stilting dressed in a black tuxedo, shirt unbuttoned, bow-tie hanging out of his jacket pocket. Mrs. Stilting in a mink coat carrying a small, high pitched, yapping, rat dog with tearful, weeping eyes.

Judge Breklandt's chambers were on the 2nd floor of Town Hall spread across the upstairs east side along with a reception area a 25x32ft courtroom including judge's bench and 25 chairs for attendees. A plain room, no pictures, oak paneling, plants, the number of which depended on Chief Majorca's having time to bring them over from his greenhouse.

My father and I were downstairs when people began arriving, an enharmonic convergence of anger, disease, peace. Judge Breklandt invited each of the shop owners along Main St. to come talk about their experiences with the storyteller. Jack Gridley, bartender at the pool hall was asked to stop by, Chief Majorca, Rick Bishop, Clancy Maine.

Once we sat down and there was quiet, the Judge welcomed everyone for making time to drop over, it was an informal hearing, some people were wondering what kinds of things happened in our town, he would be asking a few questions, he asked Rick Bishop to take the dog outside, maybe she would be more comfortable, Mrs. Stilting said it was a he, the dog tried to bite Rick, the Judge asked Edna to do the honors, Edna said, "Honey, can this man talk to me like that?" Judge Breklandt said, "Yes ma'am, I can."

The Stilting's lawyers all rose and told the Judge they had prepared, at great expense, a number of legal documents which they assured him would need to be entered into evidence for purposes of this trial.

"My goodness, that's kind of you," said Judge Breklandt, "Very productive. This isn't really a trial, but please leave them with Nellie McPherson here. I will surely want to read them this evening, perhaps by candlelight."

Then he asked people to stand, one at a time, and tell him their own stories.

Jack Gridley said he had seen the storyteller lots of times, sometimes with Dr. Steiner's nurse. One of the lawyers asked how they were dressed.

"Quite appropriately for my establishment," Jack replied.

"What does that mean?" the lawyer questioned.

"Exactly what I said you blithering idiot!" and Jack sat down.

Judge Breklandt reiterated to everyone that he alone would be asking questions.

Judy and Theo Adams from the bookstore stood together. They had never see a storyteller and weren't quite sure what that meant. But someone occasionally would leave in their mail slot an esoteric treatise on Eastern Metaphysics, or maybe Native American Mythos. Did that count they wondered.

Mrs. Sotto Voce had seen someone once sitting in the park talking to two policemen. But she couldn't remember when.

"It must have been when I was opening the ice cream shoppe, in the morning," she said. "Does that help?"

"And what was he wearing?" chimed in Mr. Stilting.

"Oh gosh," flustered Mrs. Sotto Voce. "I can't recall. He was very Roman looking. Maybe a fig leaf."

Rick and Clancy were co-owners of the Corner Café. The one on the corner they said. And being policemen in addition, they didn't really have time to run around looking for storytellers.

Vageli stayed put to voice the opinion that this was all nonsense!

At this point Judge Breklandt took a moment to remind the Stiltings for purposes of this gathering, their comments were neither germane nor requisite. Their presence was a courtesy extended them by the people of our town, himself, Mayor Thimble, my father.

Fox Friedle had the antique store. He didn't come to the meeting, but sent a lovely note saying he didn't actually sell any books and reminded everybody of the free tea and cookies he had set out for all next week and every other week-end through Thanksgiving.

Mitzy Gold was in Albany buying replacement parts for her coffee roaster. It broke down last Wednesday and she had to close the coffee shop for a few days.

After Mr. Friedle's letter was read, Judge Breklandt told everyone to take a few minutes, stretch legs, walk around the park, enjoy the nice weather. He asked my father, me, one of the lawyers to come to his chambers, "talk a bit." We all sat down. First he wanted to know whether the chauffeur had bothered me and Kathryn when he was in town. Then said,

"Do you know why I want to talk to you?"

"Because of the storyteller," I said.

"Yes, that's right. Your father told me it was all right, but only if you want. If you don't want you say so. Silence is often a better answer than talk. Now you know the storyteller? You've seen him?"

I nodded.

"Do you like him? He's a nice person? You talk about things?"

"No?" I looked at my father. "I don't talk with the storyteller. He only talks to my dad."

"Your father comes with you?"

"He takes me when he goes around to the buildings he has. To see if everything's all right."

"Where is the storyteller?"

"He's across the street, upstairs on top of the stores. I go in the light. They tell you beautiful is always there. Far away isn't far. My dad always says, 'Come back when you're ready.' Sometimes I don't know if I'm ready and the stories tell me."

I told Judge Breklandt about the things I saw, how I could understand what Mrs. Sotto Voce's mother said about me, after I went in the light we had ice cream, then my mother showed me the record books. My father told me, for the storyteller, inside was outside, so he wore his baker's apron to the light. I loved Kathryn. She could be a storyteller. The old man said she went dancing with the storyteller over to the pool hall where the lady took off her clothes." When I stopped Judge Breklandt said,

"Thank you sir. Very helpful. It all sounds quite educational. Now, do you see the storyteller anywhere else?"

I looked at my father. I thought I was in trouble. My father just nodded a smile to me.

"Sometimes," I said quietly. Judge Breklandt was always grumpy. I think his back hurt. I liked him. My father liked him.

"Where is that?" he asked.

"In the park. He sits under a big tree and talks to the policemen. On Sunday morning when everyone is at church. Then he is up and skips over to his story place, my dad's place."

The lawyer started talking. "You have to…

Judge Breklandt leaned over, told him softly,

"You need to be quiet, son." Then to my father and me,

"Let's just all go over and see this wonderful place for ourselves."

Most people had to get back to their shops, families, more important things. My father and I, Judge Breklandt, Chief Majorca, Mayor Thimble trailed by the Stiltings without the dog, 3 lawyers, chauffeur crossed Main to my father's property where he removed the padlock from the door of Joseph's home. Vageli, Mrs. Sotto Voce, the old man sat sipping tea in front of the five and dime, oblivious to events two doors down.

The Stiltings were first, pushing through the group, racing upstairs. We could hear them screaming, my father and I, as we came last into the space, dark but for a faint light coming through the dust covered windows overlooking Main St. The smell of rot, mold, damp. The sounds of kitchens, clatter, cash registers, cars from below. All the stories, gone.

Between (cont'd)

Across Sheard east from our house began a forest of white pine rising slowly 523ft before dropping down into farmland a mile and half away. Among the 150yr old evergreens were deciduous stands of oak and maple. There I constructed my tree houses, 3 of them. Below the house, yard, west, opening onto Main, my father had converted a garage into his wood working shop. I found the lumber, tools to build bracing, floor, railing, ladder for each. Two of them had corrugated steel roofing that the old man helped me to carry along the woodland trails I often walked before with my mother and Kathryn.

"Why are people so mean?" I asked him.

"Inappropriately placed in time/space," he said.

I thought it marvelous, the old man's distain for superlatives. I had come across displays of minimalism in my travels. Even at my age I could see the utility, simplicity, fragility of it.

"My mom said people are mean because Love refuses them power. They stop loving."

"Could be."

Missy Phleece was the woman who took off her clothes at Jack Gridley's pool hall. She came to town hall to visit Mrs. Heartfeldt, Mayor Thimble's secretary. They were friends. Miss Phleece gave my father a pair of Bausch & Lomb U.S. Navy Binoculars, would he please give them to me. They were her father's. He had been killed in the Ardennes Forest in France before I was born. She thought he would like me to have them.

For those I built my first tree house, south in the forest, no roof. I watched for the creatures in my dream, under the pond, before direction left itself to the company of incomplete thoughts, spherical justice, radiant, well bent by an incompetent logic. I called out my promise. I could tell their story, name no consequence, give no reason, lift no hope by my action. In my weakness I would protect them, dream survive as breath to play.

My father told me children were to play, have fun, run everywhere. To learn well you must be in motion. Only in motion can we perceive an idea in its entirety. Truth is a whole thing, not pieces of life we bite off and chew on for pleasure.

The truth was I needed a job. I had become somewhat belligerent in my quest for understanding. An arrogance one must pay for with money.

Sky & Telescope Magazine was guide to my most personal insistence. I needed a Thompson 3.5in Skyscope Newtonian reflector. A Springfield Weather Strip with thermometer, barometer, hygrometer. Anemometer, weather vane, rain & snow gauges I could get from Ben Sunny at Franz's hardware store. He was only 25 since growing up on a dairy farm 3 miles west of town hall. His dad, for whom the store was named, taught him how to fix tractors, trucks, combines, manure spreaders, how to install a milking system, milk coolers. He knew plumbing, electricity; he could build a house; he could build a barn. He said I should call him Ben. My estimation. I needed $50.

I worked for the Cortlandts in their grocery store on the corner of Henry George St and Emelie. Dev Cortlandt taught me how to stock shelves, keep inventory, operate the cash register, how to clean everything. She said it was extremely important to keep a clean shop, especially a grocery, because people would eat what they bought there and had a right to know everything was safe for ingestion. Robin had me help sometimes with his butchering. It was very important that his tools and knives were spotlessly clean. I got to wear an apron. On Tuesdays and Saturdays I made deliveries to older people, mothers with lots of kids, using a Red Flyer Mrs. Cortlandt kept in the store. I worked 2-3hrs a day, Mon-Sat, for 50¢/hr. After 3 months I had my $50 with extra for astronomical charts, books about weather, a farmer's almanac. These I found in Judy and Theo Adams' bookstore. I liked working. I liked making money. So I kept my job for another 2yrs. The last year I made $1.00/hr.

Sometimes the old man came to the tree houses. He stayed with me in all of them. But the one he most approved of was the 'Sky House' he called it. Atop the rising falling woodland, my observatory weather station.

Here he began the stories of "Where am I", "What am I", "Who am I", which are the statement/questions of human beings. He said the two statement/questions of Spirit are, "How am I", "Am I that which will be chosen". These explained all creation and natural law, so included free will, the sentience of each thing, "language is the movement by which we may approach love." He told me existence is like one of my mother's blueberry pancakes. You begin browning one side, that side bubbles and breathes up through the other, there comes a moment when the whole universe flips, it becomes itself again. Blueberries are the windows between 'time' and 'not time'. No one knows why pancakes are made, or why we continue to make them. Knowing doesn't make the pancakes taste any less good.

Away from paths, on the N.E. downward slope of timberland, I built high above the forest floor a third arboreal refuge. Music and Color. The railing with its pickets I painted N-sky blue, E-glossy red, S-bright orange, W-deep yellow/gold. A turquoise Kokopelli, 5in tall, played on the railing west. I carried an Andean G major Quena, a Peruvian Zampara Bamboo Panpipe. I had learned to play in the 'stories'. The instruments were from my father's collection of South American flutes. He and my mother often played together. The old man also gave me a Kokopelli flute his great-great grandfather had played as a boy 150 years ago and 365 feet off the desert floor in the 'Sky City' of Acoma. For two years I carried it in a soft leather case everywhere I went. The old man said it returned home to the end of time with my song in its wood.

I hung feeders from the roof. When I played well, birds came, sat in silence. When I stopped, a complexity of simple harmonies cascaded down upon my thought. There was mysterious laughter in this broken offering. There was crystal, accidental quartz, granite, obsidian. A cancer of hope, language without promiscuity, clarity, the single prerequisite answered itself from some peaceful death. One soft acquiescence released from questions without answers.

The old man's grandson, Sonny Night, was 18, drove a 5,000 gallon, straight chassis milk truck each day to the 13 dairy farms around Fulton County, pumped the morning and previous evening's milking from 300gal, stainless steel cooling vats into the truck. In the coolers a great paddle constantly stirred the milk, swirling it to prevent separation, more important, holding a constant temperature of 4°c evenly throughout. The farmers each milked 40 head, Holstein, some Guernsey, twice a day.

Sonny often took me with him. He was funny. He liked driving fast. We rolled down the windows, raced around the countryside filling the truck with milk, could hear it sloshing back and forth in the tank while Sonny negotiated curves and corners of county roads. There were always a gallon jug of cold water, deer jerky, juicy fruit gum in the cab. And each run ended in Persitch, 7mi away. 513 people lived there, including Christie. While the truck was drained, cleaned, sterilized, we walked over to her country store where she kept for us in her cooler a loaf of white bread, summer sausage, and a pitcher of milk fresh from the collection center. In warm weather Christie came out and we sat visiting on her front porch.

Three miles NW of us, in another town, Pleasant, home to 1,261 people, was the Tarragon Movie House. Sonny took the old man and me to see a double bill, "Forbidden Planet" and "The Day the Earth Stood Still". We also learned Mrs. Jensen was having twins. So, soon the population would be 1,263.

....

My mother didn't need me close to home so much. When I wasn't in one of the shops around Town Hall & Courthouse, I sat in my trees thinking, I went to work. I hiked county roads, staying to help in barns and fields on land where Sonny gathered milk. I listened.

I realized I was sad. I wasn't unhappy. I had so much. So many people helped me, talked to me, told me wonderful things. I was sad. And I had been for a long time.

I walked down the east forest out into the fields. Along the Walawala. Toads, frogs, baby snapping turtles, painted turtles, blanding, otters and muskrats, I saw a red fox, deer thinking which way is best, Christie's cousin, Elwin, had a dairy farm there, he drove a big rig, kept buffalo. In a crystal clear hollow, where the creek widened, I sank down, kept my breath, naked, swam against the stream, not moving, within movement, floating, motionless, minnows darted back, then away, around to my side, they whispered wide secrets, careening off silt and soft clarity, cold, cold, that you never felt so warm. This was hope. I didn't want to be sad. It wasn't necessary.

Window

I came in the back screen door. It banged clothes to the kitchen greeting. My mother pulled her hands from warm, soapy water, dried them on her apron. She washed dishes before she played, like kneading bread before you speak.

"Go down and see your father. He needs your help," she said.

I came running down Main. My father left me, graced to the park where Joseph danced, the policemen, lost, the "as always" tree shaking this and that, here and there, chuckle-headed, many things were confused to reason that truth, so accurate, did not suppose it knew quite more than chicken soup.

"Who is that man?" I asked my father.

He looked down, not at me, the earth. A single tear coursed its way down my father's right cheek. He was left-handed. Now he looked at me.

"He's my brother, Joseph."

We watched, still, elated.

"That's my name," I said.

"Yes."

Joseph came skipping across the park, almost a misquote. That this dance was important, no one knew.

"I've been making stories," I said.

"Yes, I know. That's why I came back. Hurry. You need more light."

Joseph leaped up the stairs. I tried to imitate his stride, my father coming after.

Joseph stood, in his apron, both arms wide to the pieces of light.

"Choose."

"Come back when you're ready," my father said.

I guessed toward one of the pieces and moved slowly into the light. There was a young woman, a few years older, painting a window on the darkness. She turned to me.

"How's it going, cowboy?"

As I watched, the attic filled in around us. I saw our maple tree staring expectantly through the pain.

"Where did you go?"

"Come on," she said, gently opened the window.

Visit

"Are you listening?" asked José.

"Sure."

"What did I say?"

"You don't know? You were talking about flowers in spring."

"I was singing! "Moon over Miami."

"Why? The moon is over China."

José and Two-Step were walking along the Great Wall.

"What a waste of space," said Two-Step.

"You mean Texas?"

"No! This! Walls! They just stand there! It's ridiculous!"

"What about mountains? They just stand there?"

"They have trees and bushes, little furry things that run all over them, live in them, lots of people who aren't intelligent enough to stay away from wild animals, fossils, rocks, things that are fun to dig up."

"Beware the solidifists...

"What!"

...who presume themselves to please God."

"That's not even a word."

José went on…

"And consider the sun, which is neither solid nor does it believe in time. Yet has been brought through life as life may also. And where is the rest of the sun that, while one thing, is all others?"

Listening to José's irritatingly perspicacious solicitude of grace,

"You're a mostly pushy little angel," observed Two-Step.

"So you think the quest for knowledge and truth is a useless one?" replied José.

The Texas Two-Step heaved forth a melodious, well-vintaged B-flat above middle C, the indeterminate age of which rose with his eyes, now splayed like an inverted ballerina, splitting the eardrum, yet without malice. Eyes returning to their normal state of amused boredom, he muttered,

"It's not like you ever figure anything out."

José charmingly snapped,

"Yes, I've heard that, failure as an excuse."

"Well, you have to admit, death is a pretty big failure."

Two-Step glanced up at Big Sue, waiting patiently there in the museum to snatch up rude little misanthropes who thought public education was a good thing.

"What do you say?" he asked.

They inclined a great deal of energy, José and Two-Step, toward Chicago. Because it had the greatest display of public art in the known universe – that and the best studio musicians. They did, upon more than one occasion, corporeate long enough to lay down a tune. The rationale being earth could always use another good road song. Sue bemoaned the lack of respect for all things lithic as well as Cretaceous linguistics. José Luis Montaño and The Texas Two-Step knocked at the kitchen screen door. I was helping my mother prepare a cherry pie for the oven. My father was taking a nap, Thursday, July 14th, 1960, my 13th birthday. My mother said to invite the policemen in, then called to my father that we had company. When my father came into the kitchen the big policeman told us we needed to come with them.

"Something is happening," he said. "It would be good if you came too, ma'am," looking to my mother.

Joseph, with Kathryn, stood giggling, and not holding still, in their baker's aprons. Kathryn came over to me, knelt down. She was very serious, beautiful, exquisite.

"Never guess. Know you know," she said.

We were warm, not afraid, and something did happen. The universe flipped.

Kathryn, with Joseph, skipped away into the stories, into every piece of light, all things, one thing, always.
As they went, my sister came through them. Ghost running, darting around her feet.
She walked over to stand beside my mother.
The policemen were absent.
My father's property reverted to its ancient utility, smells and sounds, inefficacy of the light.
My mother took my father's hand and my sister and I followed them down to the street.
We went to the ice cream shoppe where Mrs. Sotto Voce had two cones waiting for us, one scoop chocolate, one scoop vanilla, and one scoop strawberry, one scoop pistachio.

"I'm in a funk," said José.

"You could be in a waffle," Two-Step pointed out. After a moment,

"You know, the sun doesn't actually love us?"

"I know."

"Just a good drinking buddy."

They were sitting in a beer garden at the Prater with Vienna. Had stopped by to ride on the world's biggest Ferris wheel.

"Do you think we'll be back in the future near?" said José.

"Oh yeah," Two-Step replied.

Postlude

I am a window. I live alone atop a structure of failure. I wait for a child
to come and open me. To both ends of an infinite light. Goes a-sailing.
Past the grief, the frameless vision that once held life in its arms and
said, I will never let you go. For sense holds no mystery to me. Doubt no
imposition. Time no division. Distance no revelation. I am but an
instrument. A long story of Love without end.

"...when i was a child i dreamt of growing up, so people would stop telling me what to do, alas, often dreams remain just that, and i regret the waste of time..."

...rush tully still lives in minneapolis with his wife, maria, sam diego, our extraordinarily large german shepherd, is doing well, but we lost our beautiful cat, clarabelle kitty schumann, the grown children, kristel, michael, willy continue to thrive and shine in all their endeavors, maria abides as leader, rush the "sherpa for love"...

www.rushtully.com

Made in the USA
Columbia, SC
26 June 2023

19400428R00035